ROCKSTAR ON POINTE

A SILKEN EDGE NOVELLA #4.1

LACI PAIGE

Jennifer
Rock on!
Laci Paige
xo

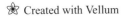 Created with Vellum

ROCKSTAR ON POINTE

Edits by ELF
Cover design by N Kroll

Devon Mann fingered a worn leather braid decorating his wrist. "Remember this?" He glanced at the smiling woman, his childhood friend—Cindy Woodley.

She looked down at his fingers stroking the band.

He continued talking to the woman he'd recently reconnected with. "I've kept it with me all these years." The braided strip made him feel close to her; she'd made the bracelet and gifted it to him for his birthday back when they were in high school. He'd clung to it for years hoping they'd find their way to each other again to see if his fantasies could become a reality.

It wasn't to be, though. Removing the leather from his arm, he handed it to her, gut clenching, feeling as though he'd carved out a piece of his soul.

She cradled the bracelet against her chest close to her heart.

Her hazel eyes full of emotion almost cut him off at the knees.

"Why does this feel like goodbye?" Her forehead still scrunched up in the same adorable way it had back in her youth, this unleashed a new pain and longing for their past.

Not much had changed with her, not really, but things were different between them.

Devon wrapped his arms around Cindy, pulling her into an embrace and running his hand through her shoulder-length dirty-blonde hair. "This is not goodbye. You're back in everyone's lives now and we intend to keep you there. Don't you go thinking otherwise, okay? This is an end to the chapter of *us* that never got started, but it's all good." He inhaled the sweet floral scent of her hair committing it to memory. "You're my friend, and I love you, that will never change regardless of who you end up with."

"Who I end up with?" Muffled words blew from her lips as his tight hold pressed her cheek against his chest.

Without letting go, he pulled back to see her face. Cindy looked like she was trying to hold back emotions, but failing. She pressed her lips together.

He cupped the fair, soft skin of her face. "You love him, Cin. You can't help who you who fall in love with."

Her brow dropped, and her mouth drew down into a frown.

Devon removed his hand from her face. She might not be with his friend--yet, but her heart was. He was certain she knew, or at least she was on the way to figuring out her true feelings.

"You're my friend, too, D, and I'll always love you." Her voice was raw with emotion and it cut deep.

They stood quietly, holding each other. She felt nice, warm, and familiar, but when they finally pulled apart, he leaned over and pressed his lips to her cheek. "Go get him, Cin." He turned her around and gave her a nudge toward Troy Bickerman, his best friend and band mate, who stood across the parking lot, waiting in the shadows.

Devon tried to pull himself together. Giving her the go-ahead to move on with Troy was one of the most difficult things he'd ever done. Even more difficult than leaving home to join the army years ago, which was an experience he didn't regret, but if he had to do it all over, he wasn't sure he would risk losing Cindy again.

Turning around, he made the walk to his car, never looking back.

He drove away and couldn't bring himself to see what was happening in the rearview mirror. It would've been that much more painful. Devon knew Cindy loved Troy in a way she could never love him, so this is why he left her with him.

He probably could've started something serious with her, but she wouldn't've been happy. So, he selflessly pushed his friends together, and gave them his blessing. All he wanted was her happiness.

Two years ago to the day, Devon had finally said goodbye to any kind of romantic relationship with Cindy Woodley. However, in that time, he had to see her more often than he could cope with.

Cindy and his best friend Troy married; she had quit her job as a flight attendant and toured with their band, Sinful Souls. When they weren't touring, she and Troy lived on the same block as Devon. He got along with them well enough, and as minimally as he could, all things considered, but it was too damn much, too damn close, making life beyond painful for him. He tried to rub the ache in his temples away as he stared at the television.

They'd started out as a garage band back in high school. Devon was the lead singer, Troy the lead guitarist, Barry Altman the drummer, Zachary McDaniel on the keyboard. Breck Adams, on bass, had joined on with them a few years ago. Who could've guessed how popular they'd become?

"Fuck me." Devon sighed, running his hand across the scruff on his face.

They were still on their game all these years later, and that was the one thing that kept Devon going most days. He stayed sober when he had to be presentable for business, or for when he had to perform, but on his days off, he got fucked-up.

And he fucked.

The latest example of which was the nameless brunette running around his place naked gathering her clothes.

Devon would hook up with anyone he could, which wasn't difficult, since there were always groupies around, and he didn't discriminate. If there was a warm willing female, he'd give it a go, didn't matter her looks, size, status, or anything.

In the past, Devon had a rep for being a man-whore, but that hadn't been the case at all. He had gone for the occasional one-night stand, and let chicks hang all over him at after-parties, but later he'd go to the tour bus, or to his hotel room, alone.

Nowadays, he *was* a man-whore, and he didn't give a shit. It was easy with his status and good looks; cropped, dark-brown hair, medium brown eyes, and a decent body with a tattoo here and there. The tats got a lot of attention. Not the reason he got them, but it worked in his favor.

He'd showered, made breakfast, taken something for his headache, and now sat on his couch drinking a beer.

The front door opened, and no surprise, his band mate Breck walked in. The guy was always checking up on him. It used to piss him off, but he'd gotten used to Breck showing up unannounced. Devon had finally realized it was nice to have someone who understood and cared. He nodded a greeting.

"Hey, man. Let's go hang out." Breck clapped Devon's back.

"And do what?" Devon's eyes felt heavy, and he was slurring a bit.

Breck frowned at the beer in Devon's hand and then glanced around the place, which was a mess. "Anything's better than hanging out here."

"Yeah, whatever." Devon tried to rise from the couch, but he kept losing to gravity's hold.

Breck's arm shot out, preventing him from face-planting on the floor.

The brunette appeared in the living room showered and dressed in the clothing she'd arrived in the night before.

If Breck was surprised, he didn't show it. He gave the woman a nod. "Hey, how's it going?"

"Okay?" She shifted her weight, glanced between the two men, and chewed at her bottom lip. "So, uh, do you want my phone number?" She looked at Devon for a response, but none came.

Breck sat Devon back on the couch, and strode over to her. "Hey, sweetheart, that's not his thing. Do you want something to eat before you go?"

She kept her gaze on Devon, but answered Breck. "No, I'm fine. Thank you."

As Breck walked her to the door, his hand on the small of her back, Devon listened while pretending not to care. But he did; he hated this part. Guilt always consumed him the morning after, but even that couldn't stop his behavior.

"Do you have a ride home?" Breck asked.

"I do, my roommate's outside."

He nodded and opened the door. "Try not to take it personal; he doesn't do relationships."

Light invaded Devon's senses. "Shit." He rubbed his eyes and squinted into the brightness. Where was he? There was a 1950s Fender Precision bass guitar hanging on the wall across from him.

Breck's guitar. He was at his buddy's house.

Carefully moving across the bed and testing his senses by letting his feet hang over the edge, he inhaled.

"How you feeling?" Breck was leaning against the doorjamb with his muscular arms crossed. He looked more menacing than he was.

"Like crap."

"How much longer do you plan on doing this to yourself?" His friend was now glowering at him.

"What do you mean?" He feigned ignorance to avoid the topic they'd spoken of prior, so he had no need to do it again.

"Keep playing stupid, but while your liver is wasting away, the rest of us would like to keep the band going." Breck straightened up, looking athletic and sweaty in his running gear.

They used to run together, a long while back, but he stopped right around the time he let Cindy go. In fact, Devon let much of his life go then, but not the music, never the music. He'd surely die a slow death if he had to give up music after losing the woman of his dreams. Music was his second love.

He closed his eyes and pinched the bridge of his nose. "Fine. Whatever. Go shower, I'll take you out to breakfast, and we'll talk."

Breck stared at his friend for a moment, nodded, and walked away.

Devon showered in the bathroom attached to his room and dug through the chest of drawers next to the bed. Breck kept extra T-shirts and sweats there for just this reason. Not necessarily for Devon, but for anyone who'd spent the night.

As Devon dressed, he stood in front of the mirror and looked himself over. He was a little softer in the middle than he used to be, his usual military cut was growing out, and with circles under his brown eyes, he appeared tired, and older, like he had aged a lot in the past couple years.

He scowled at himself and got dressed.

Once at the local diner, they placed their order before either one of them spoke.

"Well, I'm here, now talk." Breck eyed him over his coffee mug.

Devon cleared his throat and took a swallow from his own cup of brew. "Where should I start?"

Breck raised his eyebrows. "Any-fucking-where would be great." The man's eyes widened and he sounded exasperated.

"Yeah, right." He paused to think. "Troy, Cindy, and I all grew up together."

Breck nodded.

"I guess things started then. I used to have wet dreams

over that girl." Devon chuckled and shook his head. "I've never told another living soul about that, you're the first."

"I'll guard your secret." Breck gave a crooked grin as he put a fist to his chest.

The server appeared with plates stacked high with their meals.

"Don't think you can skip out 'cause the food's here." Breck chuckled as he removed a hair tie from his wrist and tied back his wavy brown hair.

Looking down at his plate, Devon shook his head. "I won't. I need to work this out. I'm going insane."

Between bites Devon shared more. "We hung out a lot; our parents all worked for the same company so when they had get-togethers, we'd see each other. We all went to school together, we'd play in each other's yards after school, took vacations together, and we all had sleepovers with Cindy. Basically, she filled our lives. And I fell in love."

That was the first time he admitted it out loud and he flinched. It was as painful to say as it was to hear come from his own mouth.

"That was when we were younger, and in early high school I was always hard for her, but I told no one. Around that time, us guys jammed together in my garage, messing around playing covers." A crooked smile spread across his face. "We sounded horrible, sucked actually, but she was always there happy to support us, and making me feel like a rock star. I kept going, kept practicing. I wanted to be the best for her, so I could deserve her smile."

Devon shook his head at the memory and sighed before finishing his meal.

2

Aria Flynn was no stranger to butterflies careening in her stomach. She'd danced before an audience since age three, and no matter how many times she'd been onstage, she still had pre-performance jitters. Once she walked onto the stage, she would go into the zone and stay there until the final note faded away. Something rooted dance deep inside her, somewhere she could go to tune out the rest of the world.

After putting her tamed, red hair up into a tight bun and applying thick stage makeup, she hit the road, heading to the local park for the Performing Arts festival.

The dressing room was empty! Heart racing and mouth dry, she donned her basic dance apparel—peach-colored tights, a matching leotard, and pointe toe shoes before exiting the room.

Crossing the hall, she joined the cluster of women from her ballet troupe. "Am I late?" She frowned and nudged Marcy, her long-time friend.

"What?" Marcy never even turned to look at Aria.

Her friend was only half-listening, so Aria nudged her again, this time harder, to get her full attention.

Marcy eyes widened. "Oh, hey girl!" They embraced and rocked back and forth while hugging. Pulling away from Aria, she beamed. "It feels like forever since I've seen you, Aria. I'm so happy you're feeling better from that nasty stomach bug."

Marcy had been off for two weeks, studying and taking final exams at the local community college making her scarce.

Aria craned her neck to view the performers ahead of them. "Did the time move up?"

Marcy's eyes widened. "What? No, I don't think so, no one said anything, and I didn't get a message. Why?"

"I got here early, but the dressing room is empty, and everyone's out here." Aria nodded toward the other women nearby.

Marcy laughed. "No, you're early, but so is everyone else. Did you check out the lineup for today?"

"No, why? Who's here?"

"Girl, who isn't?" Marcy blurted out. "There are quite a few singers, bands, and dancers. This is a large event. I'm surprised you don't know."

"I've been super busy at the studio, and before I got sick, I never thought to consider who would be here. We perform here all the time." She shrugged.

"When we finish, we're so going to walk around. No ducking out on me today." Her friend shook a finger at Aria.

"As long as I'm not out too long. I need time to hit the store before I head home. I need toilet paper."

The dancers watched from the side until it was their turn. From her vantage point Aria could tell there were a lot of people, but she didn't realize how many until they walked out. The park was full—there were more people than she'd ever seen before—and she'd lived in the area her whole life.

Shaking her head and sucking air into her lungs, she closed her eyes and let the breath out. "I'm ready, I can do this," she whispered. She moved her feet into open fourth position, her arms followed suit, and when the melody began she opened her eyes.

As usual, the melody displaced her thoughts while her rhythmic bodily movements flowed with the music. The first dance ended and they went right into the next one. After a few more routines, their flawless performance ended, and they exited stage left.

The troupe was hardly off the deck when a crew of men brought equipment up.

One man ran into Marcy, and she reared back. Due to his height, she had to raise her gaze to meet his eyes. "Do you mind?" She gave him a hand on her hip and some serious attitude.

The guy stood strong and grinned down at her. "Nope, not at all."

Marcy sucked her teeth, held her chin up high, and walked away. Aria watched as the man checked out her friend's ass until she was out of sight.

Aria caught up to Marcy and let out a disgusted grunt. "Men are such pigs."

"Oh, Aria, not all of them are, honey. There *are* good ones out there, you have to find them." She touched Aria's forearm.

"Good luck finding one for me." Her words were harsh and sarcastic, but she was so sick of her friend's meddling.

"Aria..." Marcy's eyes narrowed, and her brows pulled down in concentration.

"Marcy, *no*."

"I want you to be happy, and you should try to move on."

"Marcy, I've moved on." She looked at her friend pointedly.

"No, you haven't. One-night stands don't count."

A few of the women heading out of the dressing room brushed past with their heads down. They were a tight-knit group, and although not everyone hung out together, they had each other's back. They also knew more about one another than necessary, which is why everyone steered clear when Marcy started in on Aria about her love life.

"Stop, not here." Aria seethed.

Marcy threw her arms up in the air. "Then where, and when?"

"Never!" Aria ran into the room, grabbed her duffel bag, and stormed out without changing into her street clothes. Stopping in the walkway, she ripped off her ballet slippers, and stomped the rest of the way to her car in stocking covered feet.

Marcy didn't chase after her.

3

S omeone was knocking on Devon's front door, pulling him from a deep slumber. "Go away!" The insistent knocking continued at an indecent level, harder and louder. He ducked his head under his pillow as drool slid down along his cheek.

The knocking ceased, but the door swung open, and footfalls made their way to his bedroom. "I said, go away," Devon mumbled from under his cotton pillowcase. Damn, whose brilliant idea was it to give the guy a key to his place? Oh, that's right—his.

"No, when we talked yesterday I thought you wanted a change." Breck's serious voice thundered through the room.

Devon pulled the pillow from his head and hugged it to his chest. "I do, just not today. Today I choose sleep."

Breck went to Devon's closet and rooted around. When he returned, he threw jeans and a T-shirt on the bed. "Go shower, get dressed, and meet me in the kitchen. I'll have coffee ready."

Devon didn't move.

Breck ran a hand down his face and sighed. "Are you even aware that it's two o'clock in the afternoon?"

Devon rolled his head to the side, looking toward the window. "Shit. Really?"

"Yes, so move, or we'll be late."

"Late?"

"Yes, the festival is this weekend. We missed yesterday, I don't want to miss today."

"Why?"

"God, you're wasting your life away, aren't you?" Breck shook his head, anger flaring in his eyes, the veins in his neck and forehead bulging. He left the room.

Devon played their discussion over and over in his mind, but still couldn't make sense of why Breck would be so upset with him. Pulling his phone off the nightstand, he pulled up his calendar. He hadn't checked it since they were between gigs and their tour had only recently ended.

The date flashed on the screen. He had blocked out Thursday through Sunday for the Spring Performance Art Festival. The notation read, "scout bands".

"Shit." That's right… the plan had been to check out bands to scout an opening act for Sinful Souls' next tour, which was in the planning stages.

Showering and dressing as fast as humanly possible with a nasty hangover, he went to the kitchen, hoping his friend was still there. He entered an empty room, and his heart sank.

Taking a deep cleansing breath, he headed to the coffee maker and was relieved that coffee had been brewed. That was something.

After drinking two cups and eating half of a stale

donut, Devon headed out. He wasn't sure if he'd run into Breck at the festival, but he at least owed the guys the courtesy of doing what he said he'd do.

The original plan was for them to arrive early enough so they could be up close, but since he was running behind, the all-day event was packed. He ended up off to the side, which was fine since he could at least see and hear the performances. According to the schedule board, the third group was on. It wasn't anything he could get into, so he looked for his friend. What a way to spend a Friday night—alone with the smell of BBQ and kettle corn teasing his nostrils. But he'd be damned if he'd text Breck. If they ran into one another that was different.

Breck was nowhere in sight. Devon pulled his gaze from the crowd to the act and caught a glimpse of bright, fiery-red hair. He couldn't see who it belonged to, but the style looked exquisitely feminine. Back when he cared enough to discriminate, he didn't go for redheads, he was a straight-up brunette kind of guy. This shade of red, though, was stunning, and had to be fake. He craned his neck trying to see the person who belonged to the red mane, but failed when she was swallowed up by the energetic crowd.

After listening to several more bands, taking notes on a few of them, he needed a break. Heading to the restrooms, he thought he spotted Breck. He advanced in that direction, but it wasn't his friend.

Turning back around, he caught a glimpse of the red hair again. Despite his full bladder, he pushed through the crowd toward her. There was something about that hair; he had to see who it belonged to.

"Excuse me?"

Devon turned and faced three smiling young girls.

"Are you Devon Mann?" One of them was twining her hands in front of her and bouncing on the balls of her feet as she beamed up at him.

He looked at the girls and back to his quarry, and then back to the girls again. He sighed, raked his hand through his hair, and gave them his performance smile. "Yes, that would be me." He loved his fans, especially the younger ones. If it weren't for them, there would be no Sinful Souls. Their squeals alerted others who became curious and before he knew it, he was taking a lot of selfies with fans and signing autographs, boobs, and whatever else they shoved his way.

After what felt like an eternity, he finally excused himself for the restroom. He took his time and splashed water on his face.

Despite his drinking history, he wasn't crazy about the taste of alcohol, and yet wished he had a beer or two. He shook his head and retreated from the building. No one was waiting for him, so he tucked his ball cap low over his forehead and went back to his original spot.

A few hours later, the sun was setting, the smell of marijuana filled the air, things were getting rowdy with the all-day drinkers, and the nighttime crowd was rolling in. He hadn't seen the redhead again, and this disappointed him more than it should've. He'd had enough, so he left.

As Devon walked out of the main entrance of the park heading for his car, he took in the surrounding scene, and then he saw her.

The redhead, under a streetlight, was slipping into the backseat of a taxi.

He caught a glimpse of her profile. In those few seconds, his feet stopped moving and his breath stuttered.

She was stunning… and leaving. The cab disappeared down the street and was around the corner and out of sight before he could process his reaction.

Once back home, he sent a text message to Breck, "I have notes on a few of the bands from today, hit me up if you want to talk."

Dots danced across his phone showing that Breck was messaging him back.

"On my way."

_____

4

A ria lay on the couch trying to watch TV. Nothing appealed to her, so she was staring at the ceiling when a knock sounded.

She groaned and got to her feet. Today was her lazy, do-nothing-day. Getting up off the couch was even more than she had planned.

Looking through the peephole on her front door, she groaned at the sight of Marcy standing there with grocery bags in hand.

"Lord give me strength," Aria whispered, head tilted back. Pulling the door open, she glared at her best friend.

Marcy cleared her throat but wouldn't meet her eyes. "Hi."

Aria wasn't going to make this easy for her; they hadn't spoken since Thursday evening at the festival. "Hi."

"I came by to cook dinner and to apologize for being a bitch, and I promise I'll keep my thoughts about your love life to myself. You already know where I stand on that subject, so no need for me to bring it up again."

Aria let her friend sweat for a minute longer before she moved aside and motioned her in.

Marcy put the bags on the kitchen island and turned to Aria. "I really am sorry." Her eyes showed her remorse.

"I don't forgive you, because we've been over this time and time again, but I'm willing to forget the outburst, and move on."

Marcy's shoulders relaxed and she stepped to Aria with her arms opened wide. "Love you, girl."

"I love you, too." Aria hugged her back while eyeing the brown paper bags. "So, what's for dinner tonight?" She pulled away.

"Lasagna, garlic bread, and salad."

"Maybe you're forgiven a little."

Marcy let out a relieved chuckle.

After dinner, ice cream, and wine, Aria loosened up somewhat. "Marcy, I'm gonna tell you something, and I'll never bring the subject up again, so listen carefully."

Her friend—nestled in the couch by her side—glanced over at her.

"I'm fine dating, or having one-night stands, and maybe one day I'll come across Mr. Right, and fall hopelessly in love. I'm not shutting that idea out, so please give me some slack since it's only been five months. Aaron fucked me up in a big way, and sure, I'm gun shy, but if love smacks me in the head, I'm a true romantic and will follow my heart. Until then, I plan on having fun. So, don't worry about me, okay?"

Marcy nodded and leaned in for a quick hug. "I'll always worry about you, but..."

Aria tilted her head. "Ugh! Say what you want. Purge it from your system."

"Thank you for sharing with me. That's the most you've said on the subject since Aaron left you."

"He didn't leave me, he ran from me."

Marcy shrugged. "Same difference."

"No." She shook her head adamantly. "Leaving is packing a bag, saying goodbye and walking away. Aaron left his shit, all of it, then he disconnected his phone, e-mail, and social media accounts, and didn't even leave a fucking note. He took off. If his parents hadn't been honest with me when I called looking for him, I would've thought he was dead in a ditch somewhere."

"What exactly did they say..." Marcy waved her hand out in front of her. "No, never mind, not my business."

"I don't care, Marcy. My business is your business anyway, but I never talk about it because at first it was too painful, and now it's over and in the past. But the real story I never told anyone, is that things were getting serious between us, he got cold feet, panicked, and left. He told his parents that once he got his head on straight he'd be back for me."

"Fuck, Aria! Why didn't you tell me?" The other woman jumped off the couch.

"After month three, and no word from him, I had to give up and move on with my life." Aria grabbed her wineglass off the end table and took a sip, using it more as a prop to hide behind.

Marcy's hands went to her hips. "Again. Why haven't you told me this before?"

"Your grandmother had passed away around that time, and you were pretty broken up, so I didn't want to lay my shit on you." She took another sip.

Marcy snatched the glass from her, splashing wine

over the rim in the process before putting their glasses on the table. "Aria! You're my best friend. What kind of fucked-up thinking is that? I could've been there for you. I thought he was an ass and left, I didn't know there was a promise he might return."

"Like I said, it's in the past now. I'm over it, and I'm okay."

"You better promise me if anything comes of this, or anything else of this magnitude happens, you *will* tell me."

Aria considered for a moment and then nodded. "I promise."

Her friend grinned and held up a fist, her little finger sticking straight out. "Pinky swear."

Aria laughed, but Marcy kept her hand in the air. "Seriously?"

"Seriously."

"Fine." Aria chuckled and locked pinkies with her friend, but Marcy's prolonged eye contact informed Aria that she was dead serious.

They settled back onto the couch and watched the movie while drinking wine until they both passed out.

5

A text message flashed across Devon's cell phone. "What time you heading to the festival?" It was from Breck.

"Soon." It was Sunday, the final day of performances, and the lineup looked promising.

"Good, I'm out front."

Devon swung his front door open. Sure enough, Breck was there in the flesh, leaning against his SUV, legs crossed at his ankles, and cell phone in his hand.

Shaking his head, Devon smiled. He held up his pointer finger to show he'd be there in a minute. He jogged to his room and threw a T-shirt on, and then grabbed his socks and a pair of sneakers.

They arrived early, so they had plenty of time before the first band went on. Currently, there were soloists singing classical songs on stage. The guys made small talk in low voices to be respectful to those around them who were watching and enjoying the performance.

The final soloist finished, and even though they weren't paying attention to her, they applauded.

"I'm excited about the second band. I've seen some of their stuff on the Internet, and they rock at live performances." Breck prattled on.

Devon lost his ability to listen as a certain redhead walked out on stage with a few other women, all of whom were wearing matching pink leotards. His heart beat strong in his chest.

"Yo, D, you hear me?"

"No." It was all he could say; the damn woman took his breath away. Again.

"What's gotten into you?" Out of the corner of his eye, he saw Breck crane his neck around to look at his face. "What are you staring at like that?"

"Not what, but who." Devon nodded toward the woman.

Breck was silent for a moment, and then he chuckled. "Let me guess, the brunette on the right? Oh, or center back? She's hot."

"No."

"No?" Breck sounded confused and deflated.

"The redhead." He sighed in frustration.

"Red? That's so not your style, man," he mocked.

"No, she isn't, and it's refreshing, but exactly the reason I could never have someone like her."

"Whoa! Wait, are you serious?"

Unable to look away from the beautiful, pale tone of her skin, Devon murmured, "Uh-huh."

"Why do you think that? You can have anyone you damn well want; you're Devon Mann."

He shook his head. "She's not a groupie, she's a woman who deserves more than I can give."

The dancers gathered into their starting formation and the music started. Devon focused on the redhead, watching her every move.

"Dude, how do you even know, if you haven't talked to her?"

"Look at her, man. There's no way in hell. She's gorgeous, refined, and graceful."

The woman leaned forward on one foot and raised the other behind her and pointed her toes straight to the sky. Her arms were beautifully splayed to her sides, and her chin was up, revealing her long neck.

"And flexible." Devon shot him a look, and Breck wiggled his eyebrows.

That earned him an elbow to the gut.

"Omph."

Breck stopped talking and both men stood there as the dancers entranced Devon. At the end of their performance, the women curtsied and shuffled off out of sight.

Breck nudged him. "Go, man. They're exiting left stage. You might be able to catch up with her."

Not wanting to appear a pansy, Devon walked in that direction with no intention of speaking with her. Breck remained behind, so the guy would never know.

There was something about this woman that called to him, but he'd never act on it. Whether it was out of fear of rejection, or because Cindy was still so embedded in his heart, he couldn't tell. Regardless, he needed to see the redhead once more.

He missed the girls at the stage exit, but found the women's dressing area and waited outside the door like a stalker. Did his fans who waited for the band after shows ever have a case of nerves like this?

One by one the ladies were exiting. Tapping away at his phone to busy himself, he'd look up each time the door swung open, and finally, red hair came into view. She never looked his way, but one of the pretty brunettes that Breck had pointed out was with Red, and her eyes narrowed.

Recognizing the "Where-have-I-seen-you-before?" expression. Her eyes went wide, and he prayed like hell she was a fan and would drag her friend over to say hello. But then again, what would he say? He couldn't ask, "Wanna fuck?" as he did many times and so casually with groupies. That's how he picked up women; there was never any dating involved so small talk wasn't needed.

The friend nodded in his direction, and the redhead glanced up at him. She didn't appear to be interested, there was no recognition in her eyes, and she seemed bored. The brunette smiled and waved at him, but Red dragged her away.

Epic fail.

He made his way back to Breck. The guy had a shit-eating grin on his face as he leaned an elbow on the barricade. "You get her number?"

"No, man. I waited for her and somehow missed her." The lie rolled off his tongue.

"Too bad, I've never seen you look at a woman like that before."

"Like what?" Breck's face screwed up as Devon waited on a response. The guy seemed to be deep in thought.

He nodded before he spoke. "Like she was something special."

"I'm sure she's someone's special already."

"I didn't see a ring on her finger." Breck waved his left hand in front of Devon's face, and Devon smacked it away.

"You know as well as I do, a ring means nothing. How long were you with Diane, years? She never wore a ring, and she was special to you."

"Point taken, but at least no ring means more of a chance with her."

"As if I'll ever see her again."

"You never know, it's not a big town, their group is local. Your paths might cross again one day soon."

Breck spoke confidently, but Devon doubted there was even a chance. Another dance group took the stage. They were the last one before the afternoon break, and then the bands would take over for the rest of the evening.

6

M arcy rambled on and on about a band, Sinful Souls, that Aria was sure she'd never heard of before. "You should see them, they're so good-looking, Aria. I can't believe you didn't see Devon. He was looking right at us."

She humored her friend and listened to her go on about how attractive each band member was. She was certain that wasn't possible, she'd never seen a group of musicians where *all* of them were "insanely" sexy. Aria shrugged it off and wandered to her kitchen, pulling out stuff to make a smoothie.

"Hey, want to go out for dinner tonight?" Marcy strolled in behind her.

"Oh, I forgot to tell you. I'm going out with Bernard tonight."

"Ugh, him? Why?" Marcy hopped up on a stool at the kitchen island in the center of the room. "He has awful taste in music."

"Aside from that minor infraction, he's not bad."

"Not bad, but not good either. You haven't slept with him yet, have you? I mean, you would've told me, right?"

"No, I haven't." Aria chuckled at her friend's scrunched-up face and wrinkled nose. "We've been on four dates over a few months, I think. All we've done is kiss and hold hands. He seems content to do just that, and I'm okay with it."

"Seriously?"

"Yes." She shot Marcy a pointed look. "I don't sleep with everyone I go out with."

"Where's the fun in that?" Marcy mumbled. "And you're still seeing other people?"

"Sure, we aren't committed or anything like that. How are things with Reed?"

"Ok, I guess."

Aria paused while reaching for a glass. "You guess? Shit, if you guys don't make it, what hope do I have?"

"I mean things are fine, like always. I wish he'd be more spontaneous...or something."

Aria slid a smoothie in front of her friend and Marcy eyed it carefully. "Do I even want to know what's in this one?"

Aria laughed. "Probably not, but you sat here while I made it."

"I wasn't paying attention," she scoffed. "Your poor taste in men distracted me."

"Shut up and drink."

Marcy picked up the glass of red slushy liquid and took a sip. Her eyebrows rose. "Not bad. I'd have this one again."

"I'll make a note of it." Aria was into eating healthy

foods. She didn't eat that way all the time, but tried when she could.

Marcy sucked her smoothie down and slid off the stool, placing her glass in the dishwasher. She sighed. "I gotta get home and shower, I'm beat. How do you have energy to go on a date tonight?"

"I warned him it would be an early night."

Marcy pulled her into a quick hug. "If you need rescuing, I'm your girl. Text me, and I'll call with some absurd reason for you to leave."

"Thanks, but I'll be fine."

Aria waited in front of her house, leaning against the large fountain in the center of her circular driveway.

Bernard pulled up and slowed to a stop for Aria to hop into his Mercedes Benz. "Hello, beautiful." It was his usual greeting.

She smiled and leaned in to kiss his cheek. "Hello, handsome."

His eyes widened at her greeting. She'd never commented on his looks before, but he was handsome and neatly groomed on any day. Bernard was smart and had a lot of money—he'd majored in computer science and got picked up by a prestigious company right out of college.

Aria didn't want to settle down, but couldn't figure out why she wasn't more attracted to Bernard. On paper, he was perfect for her—except for his obsessive love for jazz. She enjoyed jazz, but to a limit. He knew all kinds of trivia about the history of jazz, and it would drive her nuts when he'd share the data with her.

"I have something special planned for us tonight."

"I can't be out too late," she reminded him.

"You'll be pleased. This is something different, and I think you'll enjoy it."

Aria couldn't've been more surprised if Bernard sprouted a second head as they pulled up to a bar-and-grill restaurant. His usual haunts were high-end snobbish eateries, and the yacht club.

He pulled his car into a parking spot and got out to walk around opening her door as he normally would. She didn't rise immediately, and he stuck his head in with his brows pinched together. "Everything all right?"

"Yeah, I'm surprised, is all. I should've dressed more casually." She looked down at her skirt-and-blouse ensemble, and his dress pants and button-down shirt. They would stand out.

"No worries, you look lovely."

And stand out they did, to her mind. Everyone around them wore jeans and T-shirts. There was the occasional dressy top, but always paired with jeans. She tried to let the discomfort go because no one seemed to care after a cursory glance in their direction. She sat and leaned back against the comfortable booth seat and relaxed. "What's with the new place?" The décor was a little on the country side of things. Not to her taste, but it had a homey feel, allowing her to relax even more.

"What do you think of it?" Bernard looked around.

"Not bad."

"Great, I hear the food is outstanding, and I was in the mood for a delicious steak." He rearranged the cluster of condiments in the middle of the table, then moved them off to the side. "Oh, and there's live music tonight." He nodded across the room to a small stage in the corner where a woman and a man set up equipment.

Please don't let it be jazz.

They ordered drinks and dinner, and while they waited, the musical duo introduced themselves and started singing. The man played the guitar and sang soft background vocals while the woman belted out songs. It was mostly country, and nothing she recognized, but it was a fun atmosphere.

As she and Bernard ordered dessert, the couple said they were taking a break, but there was a friend of theirs in the house, and he would sing a song or two for everyone. "You're in for a real treat, I give you...Devon Mann, from..." The woman screamed out the last part, trying to be heard over the screams, screeches, and murmurs from the crowd, but Aria didn't catch where he was from.

A man hopped up on the platform with his back to everyone—and a fine back it was—this got her attention. He lifted a guitar from the back wall and tuned it a little. The chords he played were familiar. She'd heard them before, but couldn't say where. Maybe once he played the whole thing, she could place it.

Devon turned around to face the audience, and there were whoops and hollers, and had she let out a sigh? The man across the room was gorgeous, so not her type, but wow.

"He's an attractive fellow, don't you think? The television doesn't do him justice," Bernard said.

She couldn't stop gawking at Devon Mann. He strummed the guitar, leading into a slow melody. He was sexy as hell in his movements, and with his shirt rolled up to his elbows, she could see tattoos on his right arm. Usually that didn't do it for her, but on him? How had she not have known of this person before? Her heart was beating hard against her chest.

"Aria?"

"Uh, yeah sure, he's not bad looking."

Bernard chuckled. "You can admit it, I won't be upset."

She pulled her gaze away from the musician and toward Bernard, who now looked all kinds of plain. "Okay, I admit, he's very attractive." She grinned ear-to-ear and went back to looking at the eye-candy.

"I figured you liked him with as much as you play his music."

"What?" She swung around to stare at him. "I listen to *his* music?"

Bernard nodded, watched her for a moment, and laughed. "All the time. How do you not know that?"

She shrugged her shoulders. "I hear songs I like and ask Marcy to add them to my playlist since she knows a lot about music."

The first song ended, and Devon smiled a private smile to himself. "I came here tonight to grab a bite to eat, figured I'd sneak in and get a quiet booth, and then sneak out. No such luck, huh?" He chuckled and the patrons laughed with him.

"Since I'm up here, my dinner companion needs to get his butt up here and help with this next song."

The place went quiet and diners' heads swiveled around, looking for whoever it was.

"If you don't come up Breck, I'll come get you and

drag you up here." Devon glared to his right as the excitement filled the air.

The Breck guy took the stage and strapped another guitar over his head while giving Devon a dirty look, but turned his head and smiled at the crowd. They went nuts.

"Jesus, are they all good-looking?" Aria mused aloud, trying not to pant.

Bernard laughed. "That's the general consensus of most women."

"Wait? What band are they with?"

Bernard grinned at her, amused. "You're not messing around with me?"

"No." She shook her head adamantly.

"Sinful Souls."

"Shit." Aria dug her phone out of her pocketbook. "Excuse me for a sec."

"Sure."

Aria fired off a text to Marcy, *"You'll never guess who I'm looking at."*

"Bernard?"

"Ha-ha smart ass, no."

Instead of typing the answer, she waited until the men played a song she knew well. It was a song she loved to dance freestyle to when she wanted to let loose. Edgy and nothing like the classical music she danced her routines to, but that was precisely why she enjoyed it.

She held up her cell phone like many other patrons in the restaurant and hit record. The song ended, she hit stop, and sent it to Marcy.

One and a half minutes later her phone dinged with a text. Aria grinned.

"You lucky bitch! Where are you?"

"With B, at a bar and grill, can you believe it?"

"No, I can't!"

"I gotta go, I'll call you later."

"You'd better!"

When the couple returned from their break, they thanked the men for playing in their absence, and the men thanked everyone for their attention. The place was packed and went crazy with all the hollering, screaming, and clapping. A server came out with to-go boxes and handed it to the guys, who waved and smiled, and walked out into the night.

"Wow." It was all she could say.

Bernard nodded. "Great impromptu performance."

7

D evon and Breck piled into the car, hoping no one from the bar and grill followed them out. They wanted to get their food and leave, following their spur-of-the-moment performance. He loved shit like that, though. It made people smile and have a good time, if only for a short while. Yeah, fun times.

"You owe me, man," Breck complained.

"Oh, come on, you love it."

"Normally I do, but I wasn't in the mood tonight."

Devon glanced over at his buddy, taking in his surly mood. "Sorry."

"Just ask next time."

"You okay?"

Breck hesitated at first, but nodded. "Yeah, some minor family bullshit going on." The pitch of his voice deepened.

That tone meant Devon shouldn't say anything more, so he nodded and cranked up the radio while they headed to his home.

As the men were sitting down to eat, there was a knock

at the door. Breck looked at Devon. "You expecting anyone?"

"No, be right back." Devon put his food down and strode to the door. Peeking through the sheer curtain on the window near the door, he struggled to keep from cursing.

His bandmate, Troy, stood outside holding Cindy's hand as she stared at the front door, but Troy was looking at him.

"Shit," Devon breathed. He moved out of sight, hand on the knob, then he dropped his head forward until his forehead met the door.

Someone knocked again.

"Hey, is everything all right?" Breck put a hand on Devon's shoulder.

Without moving, Devon sighed. "Troy and Cindy are here."

"Shit."

"Exactly what I said."

"You gonna ignore them?"

"No, I needed a minute to get it together."

Breck looked at him with a frown; he knew of their history in great detail. "Do you want me to go?"

"No." It was a simple word but the desperation in it took him by surprise.

"All right, man. I'm here for you. Gonna go back to my food."

Face still pressed against the door, Devon said, "Ok." Once he heard Breck walk away, he stood straight. Taking a deep breath, he pulled the door open just as his friends were turning to leave. "Hey, guys. What's up?" His voice was stronger than he expected.

Troy's and Cindy's heads turned, and they both smiled.

"We didn't think you were home. Good to see you. It's only been a couple weeks, but it feels like forever." Troy was before him, hand out.

Devon grasped it, and they shook hands. Hesitantly, Devon glanced next to his friend and saw Cindy.

Her smile trembled, but she stood tall and strong. And beautiful.

He admired her strength, his heart thumped in his chest, and his breath quickened.

"Did we come at a bad time?"

Devon tilted his head at her words. "What do you mean?"

"You took a long time to answer the door," she said, quietly.

"He was most likely taking a shit, leave the man alone." Troy chuckled.

Devon nodded and let out a sigh of relief. "So, what brings you two by?" Lacking the strength to invite them in, he stepped out and closed the door behind him.

"Oh, sorry! Do you have company?" Cindy stared at the door as if she could see through it.

"I do." He should've told them it was Breck, but he bit his tongue and went to sit on the large Adirondack chair on his porch. "Have a seat." He motioned to the wooden swing hanging across from him.

The couple sat down, hands still entwined. It had to be just as uncomfortable for them as it was him; they hadn't spent a lot of time with just the three of them alone in the past two years. "You taking care of my girl?" Devon asked.

"Your girl?" Troy's head jerked up, and his words were on the defensive side.

Devon leaned forward, resting his elbows on his knees, and looked at them while tension filled the air. "Let's not pretend this isn't awkward for any of us, and let's get to the point. But first, Cindy will always be my girl; she'll never be my lover, but always my girl. We have a history, but you two have a future.

"You, Troy, will always be a good friend. Nothing will change those two facts, even after all the pain I've gone through, because yes, this wasn't easy for me. I can't imagine this has been easy for either of you, but you had each other to lean on. I've had no one." Devon heard a cough from the other side of the window.

Cindy's head popped up to see what he saw—a dark figure behind the curtain.

"Sorry, I've been away from my dinner date for too long." Devon chuckled.

Troy was grinning, and Cindy's mouth fell open, and then she frowned and lowered her head.

"Nosy motherfucker, come on out. I know you're listening," Devon hollered at the house.

Cindy gasped, probably thinking his "date" was a woman, and he was being crude.

The door opened, and the couple stared as Breck walked out.

"Dude, talking shit about how you went through it on your own. I was here with your sorry ass, every day, hearing you bitch, moan, and whine." Breck glared at him as he shook hands with Troy and then leaned down and pressed a kiss to Cindy's cheek. "How have you both been these past couple of weeks?"

"We're doing well." Cindy smiled.

Breck took a step back and leaned against the support post.

"So, you know everything?" Troy asked Breck.

"Yep, so trust me when I say he wasn't alone in this."

"Yes, you were here for me, and I appreciate that, but you weren't a warm body in my bed that I could cuddle with while I unloaded my feelings."

"All you had to do was ask."

Devon could hear the smile in Breck's voice, and when he looked up, his friend winked at him.

"I'll keep that in mind." He chuckled and nodded, thankful for the tension breaker.

"Don't get mad at us," Troy started, "but we came to ask you something."

"What?" His defenses went up. It was an automatic reflex for him whenever someone said, "Don't get mad."

"Have you dated anyone since..." Cindy trailed off.

Devon relaxed, since that wasn't what he expected. He'd thought the worst—them asking him to back off from their friendships.

"Sure, there have been a few women." He jumped in before she could say more.

Breck coughed, trying to disguise a laugh. "I don't think one-night stands count, and there were more than a few, if we're being honest here."

"Don't they count?" Devon looked at Troy.

"No, man, they don't."

"Then no, I haven't *dated* anyone."

Cindy's brow furrowed.

He didn't like that. "Cin, you okay?"

"I am."

"Does he make you happy?" Devon angled his chin toward Troy.

Cindy looked between Troy and Breck.

"Don't feel weird, we're all friends here." He reminded her.

For the first time since they arrived, Cindy removed her hand from Troy's. She stood, walked to Devon, and knelt in front of him. Putting her hands on his knees, she looked into his eyes. "Troy makes me very happy, and I love him more than I can explain. I want you to believe that so you don't have to ask again. I want there to be no doubt."

He considered her words for a moment, and dropped his hands to the tops of hers, rubbing her knuckles. "That's all I ever wanted for you, Cin. I want you to be happy."

An evil grin spread across her face.

"Uh-oh, I know that look. What are you up to?"

Her smile lit up her face, and he loved seeing the joy sparkle in her eyes, he'd do anything she asked.

"We want to set you up on a blind date."

8

Devon sat in the ritzy restaurant and pulled at the tie he wore; he hated ties. Didn't mind dressing up, but ties weren't his thing. He checked his fancy designer watch, last year's birthday gift from the guys; didn't wear it much, but this seemed like the perfect time. He'd also spritzed on some cologne his sister sent him for Christmas. Why not go all out? He'd never gone on a blind date before, but Cindy begged him to, and what she wanted, she got.

And his date was ten minutes late.

The server, whose name tag read Hank, came by and checked on him twice.

"If my companion isn't here by the time I finish this beer, I'd like the check, please."

The gentlemen nodded and walked away.

Not a minute later, his server led a frazzled-looking blonde his way. Devon kind of hoped it was her; she was a crumpled mess, and adorable as hell.

Sure enough, Hank led her to his table. "Your dinner companion has arrived, Mr. Mann."

Devon stood. "Thank you." He walked around and pulled the chair out for her. He didn't know her name. It was the only stipulation he put on the outing. She needed to remain nameless until he decided if he wanted to get to know her better. His friends chastised him for it, but he said it was that or the date was a no-go. They gave in.

Once the woman ordered her drink, she took a deep breath and relaxed in her chair. "I'm so sorry I'm late. I got all dolled up for you, and then I got a flat on the way, now I'm a mess." She dropped her gaze to her lap.

"I'm glad it wasn't anything worse than that." He smiled. "And thank you for getting dolled up for me." He pointed to his tie. "This is my version."

"I love a man who can wear a tie. Ties are sexy."

His smile faltered. He hated ties. She wasn't the woman for him.

"But you, Mr. Mann, have no need for a tie." The blonde's cheeks flared bright red, and her hand went to her mouth. "Sorry, I didn't mean to say that out loud. Shit, I'm so nervous, and the tire thing didn't help. I thought you'd be gone by now. I didn't have your number to call you." She babbled on, all in one breath.

"You could've called the restaurant," he suggested.

Her lips formed an "O", and she smacked her forehead. "I didn't even think of that."

He chuckled. "No worries." She was adorable. So far so good, despite the tie thing.

"Have you ever gone on a blind date before?" He couldn't help but stare at her breasts. They were smaller than he liked; he prided himself on being a boob man, although lately it hadn't seemed to matter.

"Um, no." Her voice sounded funny.

Looking up, he realized he'd been caught looking—he needed to learn better manners. He was used to the club scene and groupies where they ate the attention up. "Sorry." He grinned awkwardly. "Me either, I'm a blind date virgin, too."

She laughed. "I haven't been a virgin anything in a long time." She said it matter-of-factly, then paused, blushing. "I didn't mean to say that. Oh my God, I'm having a hell of a time controlling my mouth tonight. I'm so sorry." She buried her head in her hands.

"I like your mouth." Her tongue poked out and licked at the corner of her lips. "It's refreshing."

He knew that this was someone he would normally bring home and fuck, but would he go out with her again? That question needed to be answered before Devon would ask her name. He didn't learn much about his one-night stands and never cared enough to learn their names. It was easier that way, less messy.

As if she had a clue about what was bouncing around in his head, she smiled. "Can you explain why you don't want my name?"

He grinned, knowing the subject would come up, eventually. "No."

"Why not? It's an unusual request." She eyed the glass of water nearby, grabbed it, and took a gulp. "Ah, I needed that."

Devon grinned. He'd already drunk from that glass. "You can keep it."

"Oh no, was that yours?" Her cheeks turned red again.

"It's yours now."

"Is that okay? I mean you've had your mouth on it already. Not that I'm asking if you have germs, I mean, is it weirding you out? It's weird that my lips touched something that Devon Mann's lips were on. Jesus, why can't I shut up?" She pushed her chair away from the table in an abrupt move.

9

To prevent his date from running, Devon stood and went to her. Putting a hand on her shoulder, he smiled. "Relax. I'm just an ordinary man spending time with a pretty woman."

She took a deep breath but never met his gaze. "I need to use the powder room."

"Will you come back?"

Her head snapped up. "I wouldn't ditch you."

"You look like you might run."

"Oh, believe me, I want to, but I won't. I need to go splash water on my face. I should've done that before joining you, but I didn't want you to leave."

Devon gestured toward the restrooms and then touched her lower back as she stood. She tensed. "It's all right. The bathroom is down that hall to the right and don't forget to come back." When she didn't move, he turned to face her, and he couldn't help himself. He lowered his head and pressed a solid kiss to her lips. "There, our lips have touched, so the water thing shouldn't seem so weird now. Hurry along so we can order food. I'm starved."

Nodding, she slowly walked away from the table.

Her cute outfit included pants that billowed around her legs as she walked. The sway of her hips was probably not for his benefit; it was a natural walk, not forced. She was attractive, but so far there was no spark or anything between them, not even after the kiss. He was enjoying the hell out of her, though, but that was all. He was determined to give it a genuine try.

His date returned, and her appearance was different. "I know." She grimaced. "When I changed my flat, I threw my purse in the back seat where it remains, so when I splashed water on my face just now, I didn't have my makeup bag to make repairs. So, you get *Au natural* for now. I figured if I ran out to my car to grab my bag, you'd think I was ditching you. Which is absurd, who would ditch Devon Mann?"

"You're just as pretty without the war paint."

"Oh no! Was my makeup that bad?"

"What? No!"

"You called it war paint." Her hands went to her cheeks.

"Just a silly expression my father used to say. I meant nothing offensive."

"You sure?"

"Yes, and I think you're attractive without makeup, anyway. A small amount is fine, like yours was, understated so that it brought out the natural beauty. You changed your own tire?" He needed a change of topic; she was very uncomfortable, judging by the tension around her eyes.

The woman smiled, and she visibly relaxed. She reached for the water glass, hesitated, blushed, but then picked it up and drank. "Yes, I can tune up my car, too. My father and brothers taught me to be self-sufficient in all kinds of ways. Mom and I were the only females in a house of eight."

"Holy shit!"

"I'm the youngest."

"Wow, you have five older brothers, if I did my math correctly."

"Yes, but don't worry, they don't know I'm here with you, or they'd be here hovering. Not because they're protective, which they are, but because you're Devon Mann."

She laughed, and it was a sweet sound.

"We're all huge fans of Sinful Souls, so when Cindy asked if I'd do this, I didn't hesitate to say yes. Oh! But not because you're a rock star, but because who wouldn't want to go out with such a good-looking man?" She blushed again, but didn't shy away from her words.

"Cindy put you up to this, huh?" He laughed. "How do you know her?"

"We used to fly some routes together."

"Ah, you're a flight attendant then?"

"Part-time, not sure I want to do it much longer. I don't like the schedule, it wreaks havoc on social lives."

"Yeah, gotta be tough, I imagine. Touring is hard for me; by the end, I've had enough travel, and just want my own bed."

"So, how do you know Cindy?" She redirected his question back at him.

His forehead creased. "She didn't tell you?"

"Nah, we aren't best buds or anything, just got along at work well enough. So, it surprised me when she called me to ask about tonight." She took another swig from the glass, this time with no pause.

"We grew up together."

"Oh." Her eyes widened.

Over dinner, they continued to talk about trivial things. He was impressed by her. She had calmed down enough so she wasn't putting her foot in her mouth anymore. Conversation was flowing, she was attractive and fun, but there was no sexual pull. Maybe that was how real relationships started? Hell, he didn't have a clue, he had only been serious about one woman, and she was with Troy.

Devon emptied his beer and glanced around to flag down Hank for a refill. Instead of finding their server, his gaze settled on a red-haired beauty, and his breath stuttered.

"Who is she?" His date's voice pulled him from the woman who had turned his head on more than one occasion.

"I'm not sure, but I keep seeing her around. All I know is she's a dancer."

"She's beautiful."

Devon couldn't argue with that. He kept glancing at the redheaded woman. "I agree, but the funny thing is, I don't think she's even aware of her looks, which makes her more beautiful."

"Huh." A curious tone left his date's lips.

Glancing back at her, he asked, "What?"

"You like her." His date tucked her hand under her chin, supporting her head as she observed him.

"What? How can I if we've never met?"

"But you like what you see, it's all over your face."

"I don't deny she's pretty."

"No, it's more than that. Five older brothers, remember? I've seen that look before, and when I did, three of them got married."

He chuckled. "You're crazy. I'm not going to marry that woman."

"Uh-huh. I give it a year."

He pulled his gaze from Red, not believing what he was hearing. "You don't want to go on another date with me?"

"No, I'd love to go out with you again, but not when you're that into another chick."

She didn't seem put off, which was confusing. "What are you saying?"

"We've been here for almost two hours talking, and I'm having a good time now that my nerves have settled, but there's no spark between us. I didn't come expecting anything, but I feel like I'm hanging out with another brother. No offense, you're sweet, and sexy as sin, but like I said, no spark. You don't feel it either, do you?"

He didn't want to respond, but she waited, and he couldn't sense anything foreboding. "None for me either." He sighed.

"Don't look so sad. I had a great time, I don't regret coming at all. Do you?"

"Well, no, but—"

"Good." She smiled. "Oh, she's getting up and heading to the restroom. You should go bump into her. Introduce yourself. She's been checking you out, too, when you weren't looking at her."

He laughed.

"I'm serious, you're going to lose your chance. Go." She waved her hands toward the restrooms.

"You're sure?"

She nodded. "Yes. Go, hurry."

He stood and went after the red-haired temptress who'd been on his mind.

10

A ria waited behind one woman for the ladies' room. She didn't need to use the toilet, but needed to stretch her legs, powder her nose, and try to cool off after seeing the hotness that was Devon Mann.

She was rooting around in her clutch when she sensed someone's presence nearby. Assuming it was another woman for the restroom, she took a step forward to close the gap in the line.

"Excuse me."

A deep sexy voice interrupted her thoughts. Turning around, her mouth dropped open. *The* Devon Mann was standing next to her, and talking to her. "Yes?"

He stared into her eyes. "I saw you earlier, but didn't want to interrupt your dinner, I wanted to tell you I'm a fan of yours."

Aria looked around the hallway just as the woman in the line in front of her turned to check things out. She, too, had her mouth hanging open. Aria was glad it wasn't just her looking foolish in his presence. "Devon Mann is a fan of mine?" She barked out a laugh.

"Yes, why's that funny? I saw you perform at the festival the other day, and I enjoyed it."

She sobered since he seemed serious enough. "Oh, uh, thanks?"

The restroom door opened, a woman exited and almost tripped when she spotted Devon. Good, so all women acted that way around him. She didn't feel so bad now.

He leaned against the wall next to them, tucking his hands in the pockets of his dress slacks. He nodded at the other woman. "Bathroom's free," he told her.

Aria could tell she didn't want to go.

"Thank you," the lady murmured, and walked in the room, closing the door inch by inch until her face disappeared out of sight.

He chuckled.

"I bet you're used to that."

"To what?" He looked puzzled.

"Women acting crazy around you."

He shrugged. "Eh, I don't even notice half the time, not until someone points it out."

"See, normal."

He nodded. "I suppose. I get it, I'm a public figure, but I'm a man, too, a human being. I'm sure you get that too, though."

"Get what?" She frowned at him.

"Fans gawking at you."

"No, can't say that I have. Well, not adults, a lot of little girls, though. I love being someone they can look up to. I'm afraid the art of dance is dying in these parts." Her sad musings shifted the mood from the upbeat awkwardness.

The woman exited the restroom. "All yours." She paused by them and pointed to the door.

When the woman didn't leave, and stood there staring at Devon, Aria didn't like it. "I'm okay, I just wanted to stretch my legs."

The lady shook her head and left, but not before taking Devon in from head to toe. Twice.

Aria watched Devon as the woman eye-fucked him right there in front of her. "Wow, could she be any more obvious?" she asked when the lady was out of view.

Devon shrugged. "Is that guy out there your boyfriend?"

"Not really, why?" She shook her head.

"Not really?"

"No, there's no label for us. If I had to put a label on it, I'd say we're good friends. Why do you ask?"

"Friends with benefits?"

"That's a personal question."

"One you're not denying."

She dropped her gaze.

He pushed off the wall and stepped toward her. "I'm sorry. Let me start over. I want to ask you out to dinner, but if you have a boyfriend, I don't want to intrude on that relationship."

"Oh."

"So…can I ask you out?"

Her heart felt like it would pound its way out of her chest. Either that or she'd faint. And then the scent of his cologne washed over her. "Uh, no, sorry, it's not a good time right now. Too much going on in my life."

He said nothing to that, just bent his head, looking toward their feet.

She was thankful she'd had a pedicure since her strappy sandals exposed her toes. They were in rough shape from dancing so much to prep for the festival.

"Can I give you my number, and when life's not so rough anymore, you can call me?" Devon sounded hopeful.

Could a man of his stature be interested in her? "Why? Why me?"

"Well, for starters, I find you attractive, and I'd like to get to know you better. And my date tonight, she's just a friend. There's nothing between us."

"I'm not a groupie or anything like that." She tried to convey she wasn't an easy lay.

"I didn't think you were, you're too classy for that."

"Thank you, but I don't give my number out, not even to the Devon Mann's of the world."

"Smart. I understand." He reached into his pocket, pulled out his wallet, and rummaged around. His fingers passed by a condom, and Aria's cheeks went hot. "Here it is." Devon pulled a business card from behind some cash. "Do you have a pen?"

"Yes." She pulled a pen from her clutch and handed it over.

He scratched out the phone number printed on the card and flipped it over. "This is my manager's card, don't call him." He chuckled. "He'd be pissed. My number is on the back."

"Your personal number?"

"Yes, my cell, and I'm sure I need not ask, but few people have this number, so please keep it to yourself."

"Yes, of course, but I'm not sure I'll call. At least I can't promise."

"That's fine, just think about it?"

"Sure."

His face lit up in a smile, and he pressed the card into her hand and held on for a moment, rubbing his thumb against her knuckles. The pad of his thumb was rough with a callus, just like she had on the bottom of her feet from dance. The thought made her smile.

It broke the mood when a few women came giggling down the hall toward them. Their faces lit with enthusiasm directed toward Devon.

A sigh whispered from his lips. "Please call," he said, quietly. "Can I ask your name?"

Evidently, hers was the one he wanted to know.

She hesitated. "I guess it's only fair, I have yours, but I'll only give my first name."

"I'll take it."

"Aria," she whispered.

Pulling away, he turned to exit the hall, but the women stopped him, asking for photos and autographs. He obliged, but the smile he wore, while genuine, wasn't the smile he had shared with her only moments ago. The one for her seemed much more intimate. She waited behind them in the small hall, savoring his glance at her every so often with a sparkle in his eyes.

11

Devon returned to his table and guilt hit him hard. It wasn't like he'd never flirted with multiple girls in one night, but these two were not his usual fare, they were both good girls. Dread crept up around him.

Things got worse when he noticed they had removed the dinner dishes, and judging by the looks of the empty, chocolate-smeared dessert plate in front of his date, he'd been gone longer than he should've been.

The nameless woman cocked her head as he sat down. "What's wrong? I know things went well with the dancer. So why the sullen face?"

"How could you tell?"

"I have brothers, remember?" When he didn't answer, she smiled. "You had a ridiculous goofy grin when you came out of the hallway. It kinda gave you away."

"Did I?" He smiled again, thinking about Aria.

"You did, and you're doing it again."

"I'm so sorry." He shook his head, unable to stop smiling.

"Don't be, like I said, I'm having a great time, eating great food, talking to a great guy. Everything's good, and I got to be here when you talked to your future wife for the first time." She reached over and placed her hand over his. "We're making memories, Devon."

He glanced over at Aria, and for the first time he caught her looking back at him. She didn't waver and kept her gaze on him. He gave her his sexy smile, and she turned away, but not before a grin spread across her face. He then glanced at her date, who was scowling.

Devon's date pulled her hand away. "He doesn't like you much."

"I see that, but I'm used to that look from other men."

"When do you see her again? You were gone for a while, so I figured you were working things out for a little get-together." She waggled her eyebrows.

"No, Aria's sort of seeing that guy." Devon gave a chin tilt toward Aria's table.

"Did you know her name before?"

Shit. How did she pick up on that? He shook his head slowly. "No, I didn't."

"That says a lot, Mr. Mann." There was a lilt in her voice.

"What do you mean?"

"You learned her name after a brief conversation. We're going on"—she tilted her head—"one hundred and fifty-one minutes, and you've never asked for my name, and you still haven't explained the name thing."

She didn't appear to be upset, instead, she was upbeat

and smiling, but it didn't make him feel any better. "I can't express how sorry I am. I feel horrible for the way I've treated you. I didn't want to know your name in case you turned out to be a one-night kind of deal. I promised myself that if by the end of the date or before, if I felt any pull toward you, I'd ask your name if I wanted to see you again, make it more personal, you know?" The words spewed from his mouth. "And now that I've said it aloud, it sounds crass."

"You never felt the pull, and I'm not interested in just one night with you." She smiled, but it wasn't the full megawatt smile she'd given him earlier.

"Honestly, no. And I feel so damn guilty about it. I find you attractive and funny. You're smart and fun to be with, so I can't figure it out." His frustration and exasperation came out in his voice.

"I believe if dancer girl wasn't in your life, you'd have my name by now." She grinned.

Devon glanced at Red as she ducked her head, but not before she smiled at him. "You're probably right, there's just something about her. I can't help but be drawn to her." He turned back to the pretty, blonde across from him. "Would you give me your name now if I asked?"

She shook her head. "No."

"I didn't think so. I don't blame you, either."

She tilted her head. "It's not like that, I'm just following your guidelines. No pull, no name."

"I know all my friends' names, and I consider you a friend now, but I understand."

They sat in silence as Devon called Hank over for the bill. His date rose, and he shook his head. "Wait for me so I can walk you out."

She settled back in her chair.

Once outside, he reached for her hand. She tried to pull away, but he gripped on tight. When he loosened his hold, her hand remained.

She led him to her car, a cute little economy thing. He didn't recognize the make or model, but it suited her. He released her hand, settled his at the small of her back, and walked her to the driver's door.

When she turned to him, he caged her against the car with his arms, and he heard her breath catch. He was playing with fire, but he couldn't help himself, he wanted to be sure. "I enjoyed our time together."

"I did too. No lie, and I'm not sorry I met you, Devon Mann."

Her voice wavered, and it killed him. He lowered his mouth to hers and kissed her slowly, testing her soft lips.

When he opened his lips to deepen the kiss, she pulled away. "I should say goodnight now."

"I just wanted to check if there was...ya know, a spark of some sort between us."

She didn't move or say anything for a moment, so he didn't either. "Just one kiss." She wrapped her arms around his neck and pulled him in.

He met her mouth, and she opened to him as soon as their lips touched. It heated things and his dick twitched, but it panicked him, and he stopped. "Shit, we shouldn't have." He pressed his forehead against hers while panting.

"Was it that bad?" She laughed.

He raised his head to look at her in the dimly lit parking lot. "No, that was a hell of a kiss. There was a spark, but not the right kind of spark. If you were someone else, somewhere else, I'd have you in my bed by now."

"Hey, I'm not complaining."

"It wasn't fair to you. God, I'm an idiot."

"I make my own decisions. Besides, now I can live knowing that I kissed the infamous sexy Devon Mann, and he rocks at it. No pun, and it gives me fodder for my spank bank." She winked and pulled away.

He raised his eyebrows. "Women have spank banks?"

"Sure, most of us don't call it that, but we do."

"What do you call it, then?" He stepped back and put his hands in his pockets while his dick twitched against his zipper. She was after all a female, smelled pretty, felt soft and warm, and they'd shared one hell of a kiss. This woman would undoubtedly be good in bed, but despite all of that, Aria still filled his mind.

She pondered it for a moment and then smiled. "A fantasy."

"I'm gonna miss you, fantasy girl."

"Don't. I'll be fine, and if dancer girl doesn't work out, tell Cindy to call me."

He nodded and stepped farther away from the car.

She unlocked the door, got inside, and while starting the motor, she rolled down her window.

"Get home safe," he told her.

"I will. I have standing orders to call Cindy when I arrive."

"Good."

"Don't worry, I won't disclose anything that happened. I already told her I wouldn't."

"Thank you."

She smiled and drove off into the night.

"If you don't call him, I will." Marcy tried to grab Devon's card out of Aria's hand as they sat together on the couch. "I can't believe Devon Mann gave you his fucking phone number, his own personal line!"

"You will not call him!" Aria jumped up off the couch and ran behind it. "He just gave it to me yesterday. I don't want to seem too eager; I want to wait a couple days before I call, and besides, I promised not to give his number out."

Marcy stood on the front side in a crouch, getting ready to run at a moment's notice. "Lame."

Aria faked to the right, but went left, and Marcy stumbled. "No, I know you'll call if you get your hands on this, but I won't let you." Aria held Devon's business card in the air.

Marcy straightened. "You're right. I give up."

Aria stood there with her mouth hanging open. "Seriously? You're gonna give up?"

Marcy nodded. "Yep, tell me how it went down again. I wish I'd been there."

Just as Aria walked around the couch, Marcy, in a ninja-like move, jumped over the side of the couch and on the way over the arm she grabbed the card away from Aria.

"You bitch!" Aria screeched and fell into a fit of laughter. "What the hell kind of move was that?"

"Me, being resourceful." Marcy gloated, holding the card in the air.

"Fine, give me the card, I'll call now."

To Aria's surprise, her friend handed the number over. "I'm gonna head out now, text me after you call him. If I don't hear from you, I will call every fifteen minutes until you tell me you talked to him."

This time, Aria dialed all the numbers and hovered her finger over the send button. She hadn't made it that far in all her attempts. The phone let out a ringing sound. "Oh!" She must've hit the button. "Shit."

"Hello?" Devon's voice sounded gravelly, like he'd just woken up.

Panic-stricken, Aria couldn't decide whether to hang up or respond. If she hung up, Devon would still have her number on record.

"Hello?"

"Please, tell me I didn't wake you."

"I'd be lying if I did, who is this?"

Aria heard rustling noises in the background. "Uh, it's Aria."

Silence.

"I'm sorry, I shouldn't have called. You don't remember me, and now I'm so embarrassed."

"I remember you," Devon said.

"I doubt it. I'm just going to hang up now. Forget I called, all right?" She pulled the phone from her ear, but before she could hit the end button, he said something. Raising the phone back to her ear, she listened and was met with silence again. "I'm sorry. What was that?"

"I said, don't go. If you hang up, how I am supposed to get to know you better?"

Aria sighed. "You're not. Remember, I have a boyfriend. And I'm still not convinced you remember me."

"He's not your boyfriend. You have beautiful fair skin, freckles dot your nose and cheeks, your hazel eyes shine bright, and your red hair is the most stunning color I've ever seen. You dance with such grace, it makes me want to write songs about you."

Now it was her turn to go silent. Her mouth hung open, but nothing would come out. How did she even reply to that?

"Aria?" He waited a beat. "You still there?" Devon's voice was more alert now.

"Uh, yeah, I'm here. You *do* remember me."

"I couldn't forget you if I tried."

"Yes, well, I have to go now." She didn't, but she was on the verge of freaking out.

"I can't say I'm not disappointed, when can we talk again?"

"I'm not sure. I'll try to call when I can." That was an empty promise, and she hoped he couldn't hear it in her voice.

"I guess that's better than nothing." He chuckled. "Aria, have a good day. Talk to you soon. I hope."

"Goodbye." She squeaked out before ending the call.

Before she could put the phone down, it rang in her hand, causing her to jump. She fumbled the phone and it fell to the carpeted floor. Grabbing it up, she saw Marcy's name on the screen. "You can't be home already," Aria accused. "I was hardly on the phone that long. How fast did you drive?"

"Wow, you called?" Marcy sounded in awe.

"I did, but I don't plan on talking to him again."

"Why? Was he a dick?"

"No, he was kind and sweet."

"Then what the hell is your problem?" Marcy yelled. "Have you lost your mind?"

"He seems too intense for me."

"You've hardly spoken to him or spent any time with him, it's too early to know."

"You're going to nag and nag until I talk to him again, aren't you?" She sighed. "Before you say anything, I promise I'll see him one more time before I decide whether to bail."

"I love you," Marcy sang.

Aria laughed. "I love you, too."

After hanging up, Aria stared at her phone. She needed to prove to her friend that Devon was nothing more than a passerby in life—or did she need convincing herself?

Emboldened, she sent a text to "Dev" on her phone. *"Hey, sorry about hanging up so quick. That was rude of me."* She sat her cell down next to her and as soon as it left her fingers, it chimed with an incoming text.

"Not a problem. I sort of understand."

"What do you think you understand?"

"Can I call you?"

Staring at the last text from him, all kinds of thoughts

ran through her mind. He was nice, he remembered her, he was sexy as sin, but her stance on dating could be a damper on things. Knowing he was waiting on her answer, she shook her head. She had to stop letting her past get the better of her. And she had gone out with Bernard a few times, but that was because he was safe.

"No."

"Okay, maybe another day, then?"

"I'm sorry, I didn't answer that correctly, ask me again."

This time he was the one who didn't respond right away. "Damn, did I fuck this up already?" She stared at her phone. Nothing. Groaning, she jumped up and went to the kitchen to gulp down a glass of water. When she got back to the couch, she checked her phone. Still nothing.

Should she reply? She placed her phone on the cushion beside her before she could do or say anything stupid. Her phone chimed, and her stomach knotted. Too much time had passed for anything positive to be said.

"Hey, can I talk to you later? Something came up."

"Yeah, sure." What else was she going to say?

"Thanks."

There. She'd done it, she'd scared him away. "Way to go." She tossed her phone on the table next to her and fell back against her sofa with a groan.

Even though she didn't think it was a good idea to talk to him again, here she was thirty minutes later, wanting to see him again.

After sitting and stewing for a whole two minutes, Aria jumped up and ran to her room to change her clothes. She needed to dance off her frustration.

13

An hour later, after dealing with the phone call from a local radio station about interviewing the band, Devon pulled up his texts with Aria. After reading through it again, he ran a hand down his face. The conversation hadn't gone as planned—it sounded like he was giving her the brush-off, and she hadn't argued.

Maybe it was the universe telling him to forget her and walk away. When she danced at the venue, she was poised, elegant, and beautiful. Then there was the sight of her in the restaurant, with her red hair—not in a neat bun— flowing down her back in loose curls, and damn the universe, he wanted to give it another try.

"Can I call you now?" Might as well test the waters.

There was no response, but it had been over an hour, she might be busy with something else. Or she was blowing him off.

Tossing his phone to the side, he stared at his guitar leaning against the chair where he sat. He was working on a new song, well, he was always working on something new, but this one? The end eluded him. Troy had written the vocals, and Devon had promised to experiment with an idea he had on his guitar, but it had been a while since they discussed it. He should've done it sooner rather than later. Unfortunately for him, that meant he needed to meet up with Troy again to get back on track, and soon.

His phone beeped, and his heart rate increased. Was it Aria?

Her name was on the screen and he was almost afraid to open the message. Taking a deep breath, he swiped the screen.

"Better yet, come visit me?"

He didn't hesitate. *"Where?"*

"I'm at the dance studio over on Stonebridge Rd."

"I know the place, be there soon."

He jumped up, grabbed his keys, and took off for the studio. Arriving in record time, he sat in the car to calm himself, not wanting to appear overzealous as he felt. She was a little unsure around him, so he needed to take it slow.

Slow wasn't something he was used to, but he'd try, for her.

Devon had parked in the parking lot in the back of the building, so he walked to the entrance around the front. Seeing the "Closed" sign he hesitated, but then he tried the door. It opened, and a bell chimed.

Music drew him through the clean, lemon-scented hallway where he glimpsed red hair flashing by through a doorway. Aria's appearance was nothing like the other times he'd seen her—on stage in costume or at the restaurant all dressed up.

She was across the room, barefoot in a tank top and

boy shorts, and damn, she was sexy as hell. Her fiery hair stood in a messy ponytail on top of her head, swinging around with her every movement causing a few more hairs to escape. Most people would probably call her a hot mess, but he'd never seen a more beautiful woman. She was in her element, and it shone from within, reflective in her movements.

The tune was slow, and she danced through a sequence of steps, but then she faltered. He figured she'd spotted him, but instead of looking his way, she threw her head back to stare at the ceiling. She paused a moment, her foot tapped to the rhythm, and then she moved into the sequence again, only to stop at the same spot. She fisted her hands and dropped her chin to her chest.

"Hello?" He knocked on the doorframe.

Aria swiveled her head and her eyes widened in surprise. "I'm sorry, I didn't hear the door. You got here quick."

He walked toward her. "Hope it's all right I let myself in."

She walked past him and held up a finger. She stopped the music, and then walked out of the room.

He followed and watched as she locked the front door. "No one else coming in today?"

"No, that's why I invited you here. I wanted to chat, this place is neutral, and no one's here to bother us."

"How do you know no one will come in?" He glanced at the door.

"I own the place." She said it matter-of-factly. "It used to belong to my parents. Come." Turning, she led them back to the room where she had been dancing. "Mom and Dad attended the same performance school in college, they paired them up a lot, and that's all she wrote. They're still together today. I'm an only child, so when they went into semi-retirement, they gave me this place."

"Semi-retirement?"

"They moved out of state for warmer pastures." She laughed. "But they couldn't stay away from teaching. They opened a small studio where they are now and teach part-time."

"I understand. If I ever stop performing live, I won't stop making music. It's in my blood."

"Exactly."

"So, what were you working on when I came in?"

"Saw that, huh?" The corner of her mouth tilted up. "The dance is for my young-adult class, I'm working out some choreography for their annual dance performance. Can't quite decide on the final sequence."

"Do you need to keep at it?"

"No. I was just killing time and burning off steam."

"Something wrong?"

"Not exactly. Let me change clothes and we can go to the break room and talk."

"I'd rather watch you dance." He leaned against the wall.

She laughed, but when he didn't join in, she stopped. "Seriously?"

"Yeah, I'm serious."

She shook her head. "If you're for real, then okay."

"I'm for real. Promise."

She headed over to her phone that was set up in a dock and tapped the screen.

When the first notes of the music echoed through the room, he assumed she played that song to impress him.

"Nice song," he hollered. The volume was louder than before.

She halted her movements and turned to him, her forehead wrinkled. "What do you mean?" The blank expression on her face showed she had no clue it was his song.

Instead of answering her, when the vocals started, he joined in, and her face lit up in recognition. She walked over to him.

After he sang the chorus his voice trailed off.

"I never knew."

"Knew what?"

"That this song was by Sinful Souls."

"Actually, it's one of the few I wrote and recorded on my own."

"Oh." She stared at him for a moment and then her mouth popped open. "It's about Cindy, isn't it?"

Now, that threw him off. "Do you know Cindy?"

"No, but my best friend is obsessed with you guys, so I hear all the gossip she reads in the rags. She knows you guys inside and out."

Devon shook his head. "Or she thinks she does. Never believe what you read, okay?"

"So, it isn't about losing her?"

14

A flash of pain crossed his face, and then he schooled it into something more jovial, or at least tried to, but Aria could tell it was forced. "I'm sorry, I shouldn't have asked." She put a hand on his forearm. Normally she wasn't one to touch people, but there was this need to comfort him.

"No, it's fine." He glanced down at her hand, and she let go of him. "Turn the music off for a minute?"

Aria turned and walked across the room to tap the mute button on her phone. "Funny, half the songs on my private playlist are ones I had my friend, Marcy, add on for me. I'm no techie, and don't have a clue, and I also don't follow mainstream music. I'm more into oldies and classics. When I hear something I like, I ask Marcy to add it."

"Why did you ask for this song?"

Aria pointed at the floor where a mat was laid out in front of a wall of mirrors. "I need to sit for this."

They sat facing one another, their knees inches apart. Aria took a deep breath. "When I first heard it, I could relate. People interpret songs differently, but to me this one is about giving up someone not because you want to, but because you have to." She gave him a small smile when he nodded.

"That's pretty much what it is."

"You gave up Cindy for Troy." She guessed it from the lyrics, and from what Marcy had told her.

Devon lowered his head. "Yes. She loved him more, and I wanted her to be happy. You know the saying...If you love something—"

"Set it free," she finished for him. "I'm sorry."

"It is what it is. I'm trying to move on now."

"That happened a long time ago, though." His head popped up and his gaze bore into hers. "Sorry, I shouldn't have said anything."

She ducked her head, and he touched two fingers under her chin to get her attention back.

The warmth of his skin did funny things to her, heating her in a way she'd never felt from a simple touch.

"It's all right, that's the truth. Few people have called me on it, though."

"Again, I'm sorry."

"You said you could relate to my song?"

"I guess if you're spilling the truth, I owe it to you."

Devon smiled. "That'd be nice."

"Here goes. My boyfriend proposed to me a couple years ago, but after a short time, he took off. He said he had cold feet and needed time to think."

"What happened after that?" He prompted her when she went silent.

"I never heard from him again." Her voice was a whisper but seemed loud in the quiet room.

Devon reached out and took her hands in his. "Jesus! I'm sorry that happened to you."

"Yeah, me too. I loved him. Still do in some sick twisted way."

"Trust me, I understand."

They sat there for a few moments immersed in their own thoughts, and then Devon shook his head. "Okay, enough of that." She looked up at him, and he smiled. "Dance for me."

She couldn't say no, not to the sexy man in front of her. Aria pulled her hands from his, and without a word, she stood. She could do that for him.

When she felt these feelings that they'd just dredged up, she needed release, and dance was always that release. Or sex, but that wasn't happening anytime soon, although she'd *love* to crawl over his body.

Before she could decide which song to play, he sidled up next to her. "Play my song again, I want to see you move to my words."

Her knees went weak at hearing the deep emotion in his voice.

She nodded, cued up the music, and hit play. The first note started, and it hit her hard, like she was hearing it for the first time again. It differed from anything else she normally danced to. It was grittier and had more soul with a rock 'n' roll edge.

Devon stood off to the side and leaned against a support column. He was far enough away from her that she could get lost in her performance without distraction. As she always did with an audience, she closed her eyes and mouthed to herself, "I can do this."

The music began and she danced her heart out. Tears

75

pricked at her eyes, but she continued. She was no longer dancing for losing Aaron in her life, but for Devon's loss of Cindy, too. The extra emotion was almost too much, so when Devon joined in and sang the chorus, she slowed her movements to a stop and locked eyes with him.

He was gorgeous, broken, and there with her in the moment.

With the song still playing, they walked toward each other, stopping when they were a breath apart. His eyes searched hers, and before she could think better, she wrapped her arms around his neck and pulled him down into a kiss.

There was a connection there that could not be denied.

The kiss was desperate and needy. Their mouths moved rough and sloppy while their choppy breath mingled. It wasn't sensual, or sexy, but there was something calling to her, and she was certain he could answer it.

After a long moment, she pulled away.

"Shit, I'm sor—"

"No, don't be." Aria led him over to the mat again, where she sat, pulling him down with her, and then she leaned into his personal space. "Kiss me again." Her lips feathered over his.

This kiss was softer, more sensual, and as perfect as it could get. It seemed that dancing for a man was a turn-on for her, or maybe it was this particular man.

They kissed long enough that it swelled her lips, her nipples were hard, and excitement swirled around in her belly, causing a steady pulse between her legs.

Unable to deal with the ache any longer, she crawled up over his legs and straddled him.

Devon's breath caught. Pulling away, he pressed his forehead against hers. "We should stop."

"I don't want to." Her voice was steady, but with a hint of need, and it startled her. "I want you, Devon."

He groaned and pulled back, looking into her eyes. "If you're sure, do you want to go back to my place?"

"I can't wait that long." She reached for the hem of his T-shirt and pulled it up over his head. "I need you now."

They were both panting, and he was as needy as she was, judging by the erection straining between them.

15

D evon held his breath and didn't move. Taking it slow was the plan, wasn't it?

Aria was in his lap in her little boy shorts, and he knew she could feel his cock straining against his jeans because, Jesus, he was rock hard.

She'd removed his shirt and her eyes hooded as her fingers traveled over his heated skin.

"Aria?"

She paused.

"This can't happen." He rose, grabbing his shirt while helping her off his lap. "I need to go." He took large steps to distance himself from her while adjusting his bulge. Once in the doorway, he put his shirt back on, and then he felt her hands trail over his shoulders.

"Can I ask why?" Her voice was strong, yet vulnerable at the same time.

"Why, what?"

"Why you're running? You want me, like I want you."

Devon dropped his chin to his chest, keeping his back

to her. "You're not a groupie, Aria. You deserve so much more than a quick fuck on a mat in your dance studio, and that's all I can handle right about now."

Her hands kneaded the meat of his shoulders, and his traitorous body relaxed under her touch.

"How do you know that's not what I want?" Her tone was dangerously low and sexy.

He drew in a deep shaky breath. "It's not what I want."

Aria's hands withdrew.

He turned to witness the hurt in her expression. Reaching out, he cupped her cheek. "I do want you, Aria. Just not this way, I wanted to take it slow with you. Do things right."

"Have I pushed you away, or said no?"

"No." He dropped his hand from her face.

"Know this, I want you Devon, right here and right now." She pressed her body against his, and moaned. "I'm not a groupie, and trust me, I don't give a fuck if you're *the* Devon Mann of Sinful Souls. I'm attracted to *you*, and I want to get to know you better, and see where things go. There's something here between us. You know that as well as I do." She quieted for a moment. "Please?" The heat in her eyes was still there.

His resolve faltered. "You're sure me being Devon Mann has nothing to do with it?"

Her face morphed into a toothy smile. "Well, now that I'm aware you sing at least one song on my playlist, that might have just a little influence." She held her thumb and forefinger a smidge apart.

Devon chuckled.

Aria pushed him against the wall and went up on her toes to kiss him. Hard.

He wouldn't argue with her any longer; she spoke her mind, was clear about what she wanted, didn't appear to be crazy, and he couldn't deny he wanted the same things she did. There *was* a connection.

He slowed the kiss and ran his hands over her firmness, learning the shape and curves of her toned body. Her hands joined in as she now explored him. Slowly, and piece by piece, clothing was removed until they stood there pressed against each other, completely bare.

Devon put his T-shirt on the mat and laid her down on top. Lying next to her, it fascinated him with her smaller-than-average chest heaving as her dusty pink areolas rose and lowered with each breath she took.

"They're not much." Aria glanced down at her breasts.

He lowered his head and took her nipple between his lips, pulling away with a pop. "They're the perfect mouthful." He sucked most of her breast into his mouth as he flicked her nipple.

She moaned and laced her fingers through his hair, holding him to her chest.

While paying both her nipples a fair amount of attention, Devon moved his hand down between her legs, passing over the neatly trimmed patch of red hair. They both moaned as he slipped his finger through her wet silky folds and found her swollen clit.

The sound she made almost had him coming; it was so incredibly sexy.

Aria wrapped her hand around his throbbing cock, and she stroked in tune with his movements.

God, had that ever felt so good before? He slipped a finger inside her and pumped in and out, excruciatingly slow. He couldn't wait to be inside her. "Shit." He stopped mid-stroke, realizing he didn't have protection. He'd gone through his wallet earlier in the day, pulling things out looking for a business card, and for whatever reason, he didn't replace the condom.

"What's wrong?" Aria stopped stroking.

"I don't have any condoms with me."

Her mouth lifted at one corner, looking all kinds of sexy. "I have some."

He raised his eyebrows. "You do?"

"I do. Let me go get them." He pulled away, and she rose to walk across the room by the phone dock, where she retrieved her purse.

She turned to him holding a small box and waved it in the air while heading his way.

"Stop."

She froze like a statue at his command.

"Toss the box here, and while you're over there, play my song again."

She smiled, threw the condoms, and powered up her phone. The music started, and she turned around.

"Dance for me." Would she have reservations?

She didn't hesitate. After a dark heated look, she pulled her hair from its holder, shaking it out of its ponytail, and went right into a dance sequence. She twisted, turned, bent, and jumped with her hair flowing in the wind behind, and her bare body exposed in different positions for his eyes only.

He had to palm his cock to take the edge off. "Come here. That was fucking hot."

Aria knelt on the mat with him and knocked his hand out of the way so she could stroke him.

"You do this for all your dates?"

"This is a date?" She smiled.

He nodded. "It would make me feel better if we called it that."

"Okay, then you need to take me out after this."

"Deal." He lifted his hand in offering and they shook on it.

"And no, I don't."

"Don't what?"

"Do this with all my dates." She waved her hand in the air. "I've never done anything like this here."

"Ever dance naked before?"

"Yes, I have."

Devon frowned.

Aria laughed. "Only by myself at home. There's something freeing about it. If it makes you happy, I've never danced naked for anyone else before."

"Very." He cupped her nape and pulled her in for a deep kiss. "Sweetheart, I need you. Please tell me you need me too. Right now. I need to hear it."

Aria hissed against his mouth. "Yesss. I need you, too."

He leaned back and lay down, crooking a finger at her.

She crawled on all fours staring at him from hooded eyes until she was straddling him.

Her sexual scent teased his senses, and Devon was certain he'd never been as turned on, or felt his cock as hard as it was at that moment. "Fucking hell. So fucking gorgeous." He grabbed her wild mane of red hair and lured her to him. "I need to be inside you now."

Aria nodded.

"Condom?"

She grabbed the box off the mat and handed it to him.

In the blink of an eye he was sheathed and ready to go.

Aria positioned herself over him and lowered her wetness down his shaft as he held his cock still for her. Deeply seated, her eyes closed, she moved. Low sensual groans filled the silence.

"So… good." She murmured the words in a sexy voice, picking up her tempo, and throwing her head back. Her vibrant red hair went everywhere.

Devon reached up and ran his hand up and down her long, elegant neck, giving it a gentle squeeze. "So, so good."

Her hips swiveled and then Aria would slide back and forth, stimulating herself before rotating her hips again.

Devon wouldn't last long with her on top, but God help him, he couldn't stop her if he wanted to, and he didn't. It was the sexiest thing he'd ever experienced in his life; her beauty, scent, sounds, skin, athleticism, flexibility, and that gorgeous red hair. "Fuck." His hands went to her hips and he dug his fingertips in deep.

Her eyes popped open and caught his stare, a sexy smile formed on her lips, and then she looked away. She focused on something straight ahead that caused her eyes to hood again.

Pulling himself out of his sexual fog, he followed her gaze, and oh, fucking hell. "You watching us, baby?"

Not taking her eyes off their reflection in the mirror she nodded and then licked her lips with a twirl of her hips.

"Sweetheart, you're gonna kill me, I need you to go faster, or let me on top."

Aria shook her head and grinned, teasing him with a few more twists, and then without warning, she rode him up and down, fucking him in earnest.

"Yes, fuck, yes. Like that." Devon gasped the words and planted his feet on the mat beneath him as his hips took over, and he bucked under Aria.

Despite her breasts being on the smallish side, her perky nipples bounced up and down.

That was it. The telltale feeling of his orgasm hit so hard and fast it took his breath away. His body shook uncontrollably as a deep guttural sound ripped from his chest. Words escaped him, thoughts escaped him, he was nothing more than explosive heat and electricity. His orgasm felt so fucking good, he thought he'd pass out, and might've for a second.

Devon had finished before Aria, and for a moment he felt bad about it, but she continued to move and then groaned, letting out a sexy sound as she reached her release.

The performance was ending, and Devon owned the entire fucking place. It had been one hell of a night. Lights beating down, sweat dripping down his back, and crazed fans screaming up at the stage. His body vibrated with the euphoria that came with a large sellout show. But now, with the final song ahead of him, the butterflies started up in his gut, and he rubbed the back of his neck as he glanced around.

Aria had promised him she'd try to make it there for the end. The concert venue was two hours away from where she performed that night. Devon was singing *the* song, the one that once ripped his guts out, the very one Aria danced naked to during their first time together.

The lyrics didn't affect him as much as they used to, now that Aria was in his life, but it was the first time in a long time that it was on the set list. At his request.

His heart pounded against his ribs as the time came— she hadn't shown. The crowd became a blur before his eyes, and his band mates could probably sense his hesitation.

Her support to make it through would seal the deal. Plus, she needed to be there for the after party. Aria had met all the guys individually already, but he longed for them to be together as a group, like a family. The two of them had come so far in the few short months they were dating. They knew so much about one another and were inseparable.

The flashing lights and the roar of the crowd brought him back to the present; shaking his head, he connected again with the audience. "That was a hell of a ride! Gotta tell you, you guys fucking rock!" The crowd went wild as Devon yelled into his mic. It gave him a small boost of confidence, but he still needed *her*. "You've been great tonight, and we've enjoyed our time with you. We're gonna try like hell to make it back through here on our next tour, because you guys are fucking awesome!" He paused on a shaky breath, allowing the crowd to react to his words, and react they did—yelling, fist pumping, and the pit was going crazy. The pause allowed him to get his shit together.

"Let's slow it down for the final song before we say goodnight." He sat on the wooden stool a stagehand brought out to him. On cue, the lights dimmed and the place quieted, except for the occasional fan yelling out or whooping. He swiped his forearm over his head to wipe away some sweat burning his eyes.

Devon glanced at the side stage one last time before he began, and there she was, still in her recital outfit. His heart rate slowed and all the surrounding noise disappeared as his world steadied.

She wore a pink leotard, pink tights, and a flowing pink chiffon shirt around her waist. Her red hair was up in a tight neat bun. When his gaze met hers, her face lit up in a smile.

Breaking routine, he stood and took center stage facing Aria, and everyone and everything around him faded away. "Dance for me." He said it into the mic, but quietly, meant only for her, though everyone heard it.

"Psst, what's going on?" Barry the drummer asked.

"Just go with it." Troy shrugged.

Devon turned and looked at his band mates with an apologetic smile. "Hey guys, if I could get you to keep center stage clear? That'd be cool. I've got a special performance I want to share with you tonight."

The guys looked thrown off, with their mouths popping open and eyebrows rising. Troy on guitar, and Breck on bass moved downstage where they'd perform on either side of Devon.

Aria stared back from wide eyes.

"Come on, baby, it's just me and you." And then he mouthed to her, "You've got this."

She smiled, and her shoulders relaxed. Pointing at her sneakers, she raised her brows in question.

He subtly shook his head and pointed his booted toe at her.

A smile lit her face, and she laughed. Pulling her bag from her shoulders, she dug around inside.

It was quiet, as quiet as a large sold-out venue could be, and everyone was waiting. They could wait. He needed her.

Aria laced up her toe shoes and gave a nod when she was ready.

Devon took his seat on the stool, sitting sideways so he could watch her on the monitor and turn to see the audience too. He signaled the guys to start.

On the first note, Aria walked out, moving right into the routine, the very same one she once performed naked, but he'd never seen her do the dance in her pointe shoes.

As he sang, he was amazed by her elegance all over again. To accomplish that surrounded by instruments, a more-than-dark setting, and a bunch of rock stars decked out in mostly black, spoke volumes of her beauty.

The lighting technician caught on and kept a spotlight on her besides the one on Devon.

The stadium remained almost silent until the end.

Devon stood and walked to the center where she floated over to him and cupped his face, pulling him close to ghost her lips over his. The lights went out. His heart swelled, and in that moment he admitted to himself he was falling for her.

There was a pregnant pause and then the crowd went nuts as the lights came on to full brightness.

Devon and Aria blinked at one another, and then he beamed at her. He pressed a quick kiss to her lips before walking to the edge of the deck, hand in the air. "Goodnight everyone, thanks for coming out tonight, and drive home safe!" He didn't acknowledge her in his remarks; he wanted to keep her all to himself.

The three men up front threw extra guitar picks out to the crowd, and Barry tossed two drumsticks out before the crew disassembled their setup.

The men filed offstage and met up in the hall, giving high fives and hugs as they always did after a show. Devon spotted Aria nearby. "Come here, babe."

She was still in her pointe shoes and walked her way over.

"That was the shit," Zachary, the keyboardist said while offering fist bumps to Devon and Aria. The others agreed with nods and positive words.

"Did you guys plan that?" Troy asked.

"No. Sorry," Devon admitted, ducking his head. "I shouldn't have done that."

"No worries, it worked out and you guys were awesome together. It's like you've done this before." Troy patted his back reassuringly.

Devon and Aria shot knowing looks at one another with wide grins.

Everyone dispersed to shower, Aria found the restroom to change into her street clothes, and eventually they all gathered in the meet-and-greet room.

Cindy entered with Troy, and they headed over to Aria. Troy hugged her, and Cindy smiled, offering her hand. It was the first time they'd met. Devon observed from across the room, he didn't want to be there for that, he'd head over a few minutes later.

He sidled up next to Aria and pressed a kiss to her cheek. "You were great tonight."

She smiled and kissed him back. "Next time, a little more warning would be nice."

He chuckled softly against her ear. "Sorry, spur-of-the-moment decision."

He pulled away from her, and his gaze landed on Cindy's. She said nothing, only smiled sweetly. "What?" he asked her.

"Nothing, you guys just look good together."

He growled and nuzzled Aria's neck, causing her to giggle. "We *are* good together."

"So, when's the wedding?" A new voice joined them.

Devon turned to see a familiar pretty, blonde grinning and looking between him and Aria.

"Hey, it's fantasy girl." Devon had told Aria about his blind date and what was said, so she wasn't upset in the least.

Aria chuckled. "Restaurant girl, will we ever learn your name?"

The blonde turned her attention to Aria and held out her hand. They shook. "Aria, nice to meet you, I'm Janel. Cindy dragged me out tonight, but seeing your performance, made it well worth it."

Aria laughed out loud at the blunt attempt to leave Devon out of the name introduction, but it was said loud enough he could hear.

"Can we go back to the wedding part?" Cindy asked, looking at Janel.

"I told him on our blind date, that he'd marry the redhead one day. I'm still certain, even more so after that performance." Janel turned to Devon. "Her movements were so in tune with your words and the music. It was amazing."

Aria blushed at the kind words.

"So, wedding date?" Janel prompted.

Aria nudged Devon. "Well, he hasn't asked yet, but you guys will be the first to know when it happens."

Devon's heart warmed at how she said, "when" and not "if".

He knew then—what Janel had known all along—that he would marry this redhead one day.

One day soon, hopefully.

###The End###

ALSO BY LACI PAIGE

Rockstar on Pointe is a spin-off novella of *Silken Secrets*, book four of the Silken Edge series. Silken Secrets can also be read as a standalone, as can the other four books in the series. You can find them online:

1. The Silken Edge
2. Silken Desires
3. Silken Kisses
4. Silken Secrets
5. Silken Courage

Laci Paige's muse comes to life at night when her family goes to sleep.

You can find Laci and more of her books online at:

https://twitter.com/laci_paige

https://www.facebook.com/authorlacipaige/

https://www.authorlacipaige.com

37193590R00059

Made in the USA
Middletown, DE
23 February 2019